This book belongs to:

_____

_____

_____

My friend Maisy

ISBN 978-1-4063-0970-6

ISBN 978-1-4063-0972-0

ISBN 978-1-4063-0971-3

ISBN 978-1-4063-0976-8

ISBN 978-1-4063-0973-7

ISBN 978-1-4063-0974-4

ISBN 978-1-4063-0691-0

It's more fun with Maisy!

Available from all good booksellers

www.maisyfun.com

"Goodbye, Dotty. Goodbye, Maisy."
"Goodbye, Mr Peacock."

What a very
good day!

Oh, how busy
they all were,
until it was
time to go
home.

Maisy
really likes
nursery.

playing
on the
see-saw.

skipping ...
dancing ...

playing
with a
ball ...

driving the
toy car ...

Out in the garden,
    everyone got busy ...

            digging in the
                sandpit ...

Everyone played something and joined in for a sing-song.

Then came a noisy time.
Maisy played the guitar.
Dotty played the drums.

Then it was quiet time.
Everybody fetched their
blankets and snuggled
down for a nap.

They all sat together
and listened quietly
to the story.

"Once upon a time..."

Tallulah reminded them
to wash their
hands.

Maisy and Dotty went to the little toilets.

"Thank you very, very, very much," Tallulah said. "Oh, yummy, scrummy!"

At elevenses, they
had drinks,
biscuits
and fruit.

"And that's Maisy
and me, dancing,"
said Dotty.

What brilliant paintings!
Mr Peacock helped put
them up on the wall.
"That's my new house,"
Maisy said.

"We are starting
with painting
today."

"Good morning, Maisy and Dotty!" said Mr Peacock.

First Maisy hung her coat on her own special peg with her name on it.

"Hello, Dotty," she said.
"Hello, Maisy," said Dotty.
"Look, Cyril must be here too, and Tallulah."

Cyril

Dotty

Maisy

Tallulah

Today was a very good day for Maisy because she went to nursery.

There's always so much to do at nursery, and so many friends to see.

Maisy Goes to Nursery

Lucy Cousins

WALKER BOOKS
AND SUBSIDIARIES
LONDON • BOSTON • SYDNEY • AUCKLAND

First published 2009 by Walker Books Ltd
87 Vauxhall Walk, London SE11 5HJ

This edition published 2012

2 4 6 8 10 9 7 5 3 1

© 2009 Lucy Cousins
Lucy Cousins font © 2009 Lucy Cousins

The author/illustrator has asserted her moral rights
Illustrated in the style of Lucy Cousins by King Rollo Films Ltd
Maisy™. Maisy is a registered trademark of Walker Books Ltd, London

Printed in China

British Library Cataloguing in Publication Data:
a catalogue record for this book is
available from the British Library

ISBN 978-1-4063-4460-8

www.walker.co.uk